Ahoy, mateys! Do you want to join my pirate crew? Then just say the pirate password: "Yo-ho-ho!" As part of my crew, you'll need to learn the Never Land pirate pledge.

TODAY'S PIRATE PLEDGE

WWW.ABDOPUBLISHING.COM

Reinforced library bound edition published in 2015 by Spotlight, a division of ABDO
PO Box 398166, Minneapolis, Minnesota 55439. Spotlight produces high-quality reinforced library bound editions for schools and libraries. Published by agreement with Disney Enterprises, Inc.

Printed in the United States of America, North Mankato, Minnesota.
052014
072014

DISNEY PRESS

THIS BOOK CONTAINS RECYCLED MATERIALS

CATALOGING-IN-PUBLICATION DATA

La Rose, Melinda.
Jake and the Neverland Pirates: X marks the croc! / written by Melinda La Rose ; illustrated by Alan Batson.
p. cm. -- (World of reading. Level Pre-1)
Summary: Jake and his crew try to get Hook to work with them to rescue the map to the waterslide at Pirates Plunge from the crocodile that swallowed it.
1. Pirates--Juvenile fiction. 2. Maps--Juvenile fiction. 3. Crocodiles--Juvenile fiction. I. Batson, Alan, ill. II. Title. III. Series. IV. Jake and the Never Land Pirates (Television program)
[E]--dc23

978-1-61479-247-5 (Reinforced Library Bound Edition)

ABDO

Spotlight

A Division of ABDO
www.abdopublishing.com

Disney
Jake and the Never Land Pirates

X Marks the Croc!

Written by Melinda LaRose

Based on the episode "Rock the Croc" by Nicole Dubuc

Illustrated by Alan Batson

Disney Press
New York

The sun is shining on Pirate Island.
Jake spots something in the water.
"Treasure ahoy, mateys!"
It's a message in a bottle from Peter Pan!

"A map of Pirates' Plunge!" says Cubby.
"Pirates' Plunge is the coolest waterslide in all of Never Land," says Jake.
"Yo-ho, let's go!" says Izzy.

"There's Jake and his crew," says Hook.
"Where are they going?"

"The map said Pirates' Plunge is this way," calls Cubby.

"Pirates' Plunge?" asks Hook.
"Of course! Those puny pirates are going to cool off on the waterslide.
Smee, I want that map!"

How many coconuts can you find on the beach?

Yoink! Hook nabs the map.
"Yay-hey, no way!" shouts Izzy.
"Don't swipe our map," says Jake.
"Let's go to Pirates' Plunge together!"

"Together? Never!" says  Hook.

"I want the place all to myself!"

 Jake tries to grab the  bottle back.

It goes flying into the sky!

"Shiver me timbers," says Izzy.
"The croc ate the map!"
"Aww, coconuts!" says Cubby. "Now no one can go to Pirates' Plunge."

Just then, a feather lands on Cubby's nose.

"Ahh…ahhh…CHOO!"

"That's it!" says Jake. "We can get the croc to sneeze out the map!"

Can you help Jake spot the crocodile?

The crew finds the croc sleeping.
"Maybe he will sneeze if we tickle his nose with a feather," says Jake.
"Worked for me," says Cubby.

Skully tickles the croc's nose.

"Ahh…ahhh…ahhh…"

"Get set to catch the map," says Jake.

But the croc doesn't sneeze!

"Step aside, silly swabs," says Hook.
He rubs a feather on the croc's nose.
"Gootchy-gootchy-goo!"
But the croc doesn't sneeze!

“Why didn’t it work, Smee?”

Hook
asks.

“I don’t…ahhh…ahhh…CHOO!”

Smee
sneezes and wakes up the

croc
!

"Save me, Smee!" yells Hook.

He runs off.

Just then, Jake and Izzy hear a burp.

"Excuse me," says Cubby.

"Great thinking, Cubby," says Izzy.

"Maybe we can make the croc
burp out the map," says Jake.
"The fizzy water at Geyser Gulch
makes me burp," says Izzy.
"Hey, croc, want a drink of water?"

"The  croc sure is drinking a lot of that fizzy  water," says  Izzy. "Look out! He's going to blow!" warns 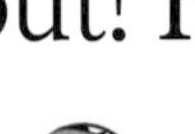 Skully.

"Get set to catch the map," says Jake.

The croc lets out a teeny-tiny burp.

"That's it?" says Cubby.

"I'll make the croc burp," says Hook.
Hook pats the croc's tummy, but
the croc doesn't like it one bit.
The croc sends Hook flying!

"Smeeeeeee!" yells Hook.

"Flap your arms, Cap'n," says Smee.

"Always works for me," says Skully.

Cubby giggles at Skully's joke.

"Cubby, you're full of ideas," says Jake.

"I am?" asks Cubby.

"Maybe we can make the croc laugh out the map," says Jake.

"A ha-ha-ha and hee-hee-hee.
Come on, croc, and laugh with me!"
"Crackers! He's not even cracking
a smile," says Skully.

"I'll show you how it's done,"

says Hook.

Hook clowns around, but the croc

still doesn't laugh.

What colors do you see on Hook's clown suit?

"Give me my crocodile net,"
yells Hook. "I want that map!"
"We all want the map," says Jake,
"but trapping the croc isn't right."

“Izzy, a little Pixie Dust, please,” says Jake.

Jake takes the net from Smee.

“Give me back my net!” yells Hook.

Jake drops the net, and Hook gets all tangled up.

"Uh-oh, sorry, Hook," says Jake.

"Get me out of this net!" calls Hook.
He steps on a log.
The croc hits the log, and Hook goes
flying. "Whoooooaaaa!"

“The croc is laughing!” says Jake.
The bottle with the map flies out of the croc’s mouth.
“Yo-ho, way to go!” says Jake.

Can you spot Captain Hook and Mr. Smee?

"Peter Pan was right! Pirates' Plunge is awesome!" says Cubby.

"Too bad Hook tried to swipe our map," says Izzy.

"If that sneaky snook had shared, he would be in the water instead of up a tree," says Izzy.

“For solving pirate problems,

we earned some Gold Doubloons!”

says Jake.

“Yay-hey, well done,” says Izzy.

How many Gold Doubloons did Jake and the crew earn?